For Andrew with lots and lots of love!!!!.
From Aunt Debbie

THE DAY THE SKY SPLIT

THE DAY THE SKY SPLIT

by

M. Lev

ILLUSTRATED by DEBRA KAPNEK LEVIN

Antroll Publishing Company
Vermont

Creative Consultants

Maia Aronson, Hal Blatt, Jenny Blumberg, Todd Burstyn, Jennifer Carstens, Natalie Diamond, Yfat Eyal, Yael Foss, Rachel Gimbel, Matthew Katcoff, Ashley Katz, Jonathan Konits, Lauren Kopp, Emily Kramer, Elizabeth Levin, Ashlie Levy, Gleb Linchuk, Beth Littmann, Karen Love, Joshua Madoff, Andrea Molinatti, Sheri Morstein, Tova Reichel, Seth Rosen, Orlee Rosner, Scott Schwartzberg, Shira Silberg, Adam Small, Emily Straus, Evan Tucker, Ohad Wilner, Michael Zmora, Gabrielle Zucker, Mr. Joel Breitstein, Mrs. Hedy Goldstein, Mrs. Elissa Hellman, Mrs. Faye Pollack, and Dr. Paul Schneider.

Text copyright © 1991 by M. Lev.
Illustrations copyright © 1991 by Debra Kapnek Levin.

Published by Antroll Publishing Company, Vermont.

Printed in the United States of America.

Library of Congress Catalog Card Number: 91-71188.

ISBN 1-877656-07-0.

To the memory of
Hyman Shanok. A gentle,
kind and caring man –
someone you could count on.

Once upon a time there were two side-by-side towns. The two towns shared one street, Main Street, which was half in one town and half in the other. The yellow stripe that ran down the middle of Main Street was the dividing line between the two towns.

Although the towns were next door neighbors, they were as different from each other as could be. One was called the Town of Wet. The other was called the Town of Dry.

The people in the Town of Wet only came outside in the rain. They hated being dry.

In the Town of Wet, the people were tall and thin, and they wore only bathing suits. They never wore shirts or socks or pants or jackets.

The people in the Town of Dry only came outside when the sun was shining. They hated getting wet.

In the town of Dry, the people were short and round, and they always wore all kinds of clothes. Sometimes they even wore goggles and carried umbrellas. Almost every inch of their skin was covered. This way, they couldn't be touched by even a single drop of rain if a sudden shower surprised them and they had to run back to their houses.

Policemen in the Town of Wet carried hair driers instead of guns
and they chased criminals to blow them dry . . .

Policemen in the Town of Dry carried water pistols and they chased criminals to squirt them.

So when did the people in the two towns ever meet each other? For years and years they didn't . . . until one day a strange and wonderful thing happened.

One warm, cloudless day in the middle of May, the sky suddenly started turning colors. It became purple on one side and green on the other, and a crackling sound echoed across the whole world. Everyone looked up and watched in amazement as the sky split open down the middle, and there in the highest heights a little white cloud appeared.

The little cloud floated slowly down through the split in the sky and drifted from one side of the sun to the other until it came to rest right above the Town of Wet. It was a small cloud that looked like hundreds of cottonballs joined together, and it was all alone up there, the only cloud in the sky.

Out of the little cloud a light rain began falling, and the rain fell only on the Town of Wet.

For the first time ever, it was raining in the Town of Wet, but it was not raining in the Town of Dry. People began flowing out of their houses in both towns at the same time, gathering into large crowds on opposite sides of Main Street.

On the Town of Wet side of Main Street, the people wore only bathing suits. And they stood directly under the little cloud, singing in the rain like some grownups do in the shower.

On the Town of Dry side of Main Street, people wore more pieces of clothing than anyone could count. And umbrellas opened into colorful circles over their heads.

The mayors of both towns were standing among the crowds along Main Street. Each of the mayors had dreamed of a day when all of their townspeople would come outside and meet each other, and here it was!

At first the people from the two towns stood in silence, staring at each other as if they came from different planets. Slowly, people began talking softly to themselves and to each other until they sounded like a giant swarm of bumble bees. The sound grew louder and louder.

The mayor of the Town of Wet, who was splashing in a rain puddle, called out to the mayor of the Town of Dry, who was standing in the sunshine, "I've always wanted to know how it feels to be dressed like you."

"And I've always wanted to know how it feels to get wet and play in the rain," the mayor of the Town of Dry called back.

"Why don't you and I switch places?" asked the mayor of the Town of Wet.

The mayor of the Town of Dry thought for a moment, then he flashed a friendly smile. "Great idea, let's do it. And let's also switch clothes."

So the two mayors not only changed places, but they also traded clothes.

And when the townspeople saw what their mayors had done, all of them started doing the same thing. In a matter of minutes, the people in the Town of Dry were standing in the Town of Wet, wearing only bathing suits and getting drenched by that little raincloud . . .

The people from the Town of Wet were standing in the Town of Dry, wearing layers of clothes and holding umbrellas over their bundled-up heads.

The people from the two towns looked at each other and called out, "Now I look like you and you look like me."

From that day on, the people in the two towns told the story of how the little raincloud taught them to appreciate their differences and how nice it is to know your neighbors.

And forever after, in *all* kinds of weather, the people from the two towns shared their clothes, their friendship and their differences.

The End

The author and the illustrator wish to thank the children and teachers of the Solomon Schechter Day School in Baltimore, Maryland for the unique role they played in the process of creating this book. In working together with them, we found their imaginations to be "contagious" – and we hope they never find a cure.